Samuel French Acting

Anatom

by Jim Leonard

SAMUELFRENCH.COM   **SAMUELFRENCH.CO.UK**

MUSIC USE NOTE

Licensees are solely responsible for obtaining formal written permission from copyright owners to use copyrighted music in the performance of this play and are strongly cautioned to do so. If no such permission is obtained by the licensee, then the licensee must use only original music that the licensee owns and controls. Licensees are solely responsible and liable for all music clearances and shall indemnify the copyright owners of the play(s) and their licensing agent, Samuel French, against any costs, expenses, losses and liabilities arising from the use of music by licensees. Please contact the appropriate music licensing authority in your territory for the rights to any incidental music.

IMPORTANT BILLING AND CREDIT REQUIREMENTS

If you have obtained performance rights to this title, please refer to your licensing agreement for important billing and credit requirements.

CHARACTERS

GALEN GRAY
JUNE MULDOON, 15
REBEKAH MULDOON, her mother
PASTOR PHINEAS WINGFIELD
TINY WINGFIELD, his sister
CRUTCH COLLINS, blacksmith
BELVA COLLINS, his wife
MAGGIE, tavern owner
HOMER, 17, a farmer

PLACE

The play takes place in Gray, Indiana in the 1800's. You can stage
this play with nine good actors, one bench, one stool, and a chair.

DEDICATION

Plays come from mysterious places – at least for me. Here's how this one came to be: First, I learned that my dear friend John Geter, for whom I'd written the role of Buddy in a play of mine called THE DIVINERS, had a disease called AIDS. Like me, John grew up in a small town in Indiana. Some in his childhood community did not react well to the news of John's illness. The dying they could deal with. The truly frightening part was John being gay. Gay equaled damnation: therefore AIDS, therefore death. The irony is that John left acting to become a minister and baptized my sons. But that's how folks thought in the early 90's.

At the same time this illness was happening to John, Dr. Henry I. Schvey came to New York's Circle Repertory Theatre seeking to commission a play to celebrate the centennial of Washington University's medical school. I needed the money. I deposited his check and proceeded to panic, having no idea what to write about. Then I had a thought: "What would happen if it was only the Christians who got AIDS?" I love Jesus, but that's where I started: The godly get ill, complications ensue. It's easy to judge the righteous – it's hard to tell a good story.

For the next two-and-a-half years, I wrote and rewrote ANATOMY OF GRAY (which I called GRAY'S ANATOMY for awhile). Dr. Schvey bravely staged the premiere with a cast of talented students. I rewrote. Rob Bundy mounted a beautiful and simple production in Circle Rep's Laboratory Theatre. I rewrote. I staged it in Arizona. It was staged San Francisco. I rewrote. My friend Steven Deitz directed a stunning production at A Contemporary Theatre in Seattle. The audience seemed happy, but I knew something was profoundly wrong with the story, and I didn't know how to fix it. So I put it away.

For ten years.

Now. Time passes, but time heals nothing – it just lets us grow numb to loss. Years after John's ashes were spread on the water, I was in a very dark place. I was depressed, I was angry, and I didn't even know I was grieving. Then one night, I had a dream about John...and when I woke up, I knew how to tell the story.

This is the truth: Craig Slaight called from A.C.T. in San Francisco a week later; I told him about my dream; he dared me to write it; and then he staged it. This time, the play was the river and I was the raft. I combined and complicated characters, and I put a young woman at the center. Her father had died, and she wouldn't shut up about loss and love and grief and sex and longing and landscape and weather. I didn't find the story, the story found me.

—Jim Leonard

ACT I

(We hear an acoustic version of "The Water is Wide," simply, beautifully felt. LIGHTS RISE ON JUNE who speaks directly to the audience. The TOWNSPEOPLE ENTER on or just before their lines, or else they are on stage from the beginning. Most of this section is told right to the audience.)

JUNE. Once upon a time there was a girl who looked remarkably like me./You know how much weather there is?/ Well that's how many feelings she had. It's like there was one sky outside her, and a sky just as huge on the inside./She was one of the more interesting people you'd ever want to meet. But nobody knew it. Because she lived in Gray, Indiana. A town which was primarily notable for bein the most boring place in the world.

REBEKAH. June/ Put a lid on it.

JUNE. Mother, there's nothin to do here but live here.

CRUTCH. Oh, hell, we got everything right here in Gray a body could need.

BELVA. Mr. Collins, there's no need to curse.

CRUTCH. We got folks to farm —

HOMER. That would be me.

CRUTCH. — and folks to fix thrashers and grub plows and broken-down wagons and such —

HOMER. That would be you.

CRUTCH. — and plenty of folks to fix meals:

MAGGIE. That would be me —

BELVA. And me —

TINY. And me —

REBEKAH. And me —

JUNE. I mainly get stuck with the dishes.

TINY. Breakfast, dinner, and supper, every blessed day, three times a day, 'til the end of foreseeable time.

BELVA. Tiny, you don't have but one soul to cook for.

TINY. I cook for my brother. I cook for myself —

BELVA. What I mean is you don't have a husband, dear.

TINY. Bless you for pointin that out, Belva.

CRUTCH. And we've got us a soul-fixer!

(PHINEAS wears wire-rimmed spectacles — one lens is clear, and the other is darkly tinted.)

PHINEAS. Phineas Wingfield, brother to Tiny, and Pastor-at-large.

HOMER. That man would baptize a dog.

PHINEAS. I always loved water.

MAGGIE. One time, he got so hepped up with the Spirit, he tried dunkin a cat. That didn't work out too well.

PHINEAS. Hold it! Just rein it in, wouldja? *(To the audience.)* The reason I dunked every creature in sight, includin the aforementioned feline, is this: I can't picture heaven without 'em. If heaven ain't much like Indiana, well Lord God forgive me, I don't want to go. But I'm plannin to go! And I'm plannin to take this town with me — lock, stock, and cat.

MAGGIE. But Puff wasn't much for the water, you see; she scratched out the preacher's eye.

TINY. Oh, it was awful. She lashed out and gutted it clean from the socket, that cat.

HOMER. I heard tell she ate the eye, too.

TINY. Gobbled it right down, sat there and smiled.

JUNE. You see there? That's just what I'm talkin about. That right there — that eyeball eatin cat is the most interesting thing that ever happened around here. *(Beat, smile.)* At least til my story begins. Anatomy of Gray.

TOWNSPEOPLE. Chapter One:

(Lights isolate JUNE.)

JUNE. In the beginnin, we had folks to shod horses and folks to fix houses, folks to fix meals and thrashers and folks to save souls — but the one thing we lacked in our town was a person to fix other people. For Gray at the time was a town with no healer...*(Beat)* And that's where the death of my father fits in.

(REBEKAH has appeared behind June, touched her shoulder, and now they embrace in quiet grief as lights bring us to a funeral, and the TOWNSPEOPLE SING:)

TOWNSPEOPLE.
"Softly and tenderly, Jesus is calling,
Calling for you and for me;
See on the portals, He's waiting and watching,
Watching for you and for me.
Come home, come home: ye who are weary come home;
Softly and tenderly, Jesus is calling,
Calling: Oh, sinner, come home."

(They REPEAT THE CHORUS IN HARMONY as BELVA and
CRUTCH tell us the story, so the singing ends up on a lovely
"Amen" just as the narration ends:)

BELVA. June lost her pa; Rebekah was widowed; and we lost
a good neighbor and friend.

CRUTCH. *(Hat in hand.)* Oh, there wasn't nothin that man
could not grow. His alfalfa used to come in so pretty that grown
men would stand before his fields and weep./

BELVA. And then one day, out of nowhere, his heart just gave
out./

CRUTCH. It was Juney who found him, still tethered to his
plow./

BELVA. Her father's face was dark blue under the white hot
noon sun, and the dust of his fields floated around him/

CRUTCH. And so all of us gathered together, like leaves of an
autumm together, to turn that man back to the earth. /

TOWNSPEOPLE.
(Singing)
"A-MEN." /

PHINEAS. The Lord gave, and the Lord hath taken away.
TOWNSPEOPLE. Blessed be the name of the Lord./

PHINEAS.   /
"Ashes to ashes —"

REBEKAH & JUNE.
(Kneeling)   /
"Ashes to ashes..."

PHINEAS.
"And dust unto dust —"

REBEKAH & JUNE.
"Dust unto dust..."

BELVA. *(To the audience.)* It was a beautiful service.

(The MEN put their hats on. People give their condolences to REBEKAH and JUNE. REBEKAH slowly stands to accept their sympathies, but JUNE remains alone on her knees before her father's "grave.")

TINY. He's gonna be sorely missed, Becky.
TOWNSPEOPLE. *(Before exiting, quietly.)* —My sympathies. —Condolences, ma'am. —You're in our prayers.
PHINEAS. *(Kindly)* Your Pa's gone to a better world, June. Don't ever forget that, you hear?

(Everyone exits but JUNE and Rebekah. LIGHTS ISOLATE JUNE.)

JUNE. *(To the theater.)* Throughout the funeral and the well-meaning whispers which followed, I kept chokin back the urge to just stand up and scream: It ain't right —it ain't fair that my father is gone, and my mother is weepin alone in her room. I can't even breathe without cryin, and nothin is ever gonna feel the same to me, ever! And I cannot believe my Pa won't see the sun rise again, or be here to give me away when I marry someday, and I would trade every feelin of happiness I've ever known just to see him again! People say Time heals everything — but Time didn't heal my father; and neither did God.

REBEKAH. So that night June put pen to paper and wrote herself a business-like letter./

JUNE. "Dearest Almighty: I don't want anyone I care about to die again ever./ Including, but not limited to me./ So, please! Would you send us a doctor?"/

REBEKAH. She wrote — /

JUNE. And make him a good-lookin doctor. /

REBEKAH. June thought. /

JUNE. Because I'm almost sixteen, and I don't think I'm vain, but I know I'm not ugly,/ and most of the boys around here are just...boys around here.

(SOUND OF DISTANT THUNDER as JUNE EXITS and CRUTCH
ENTERS.)

CRUTCH. The day that the healer arrived was precipitous, friends, in a number of ways./

(MORE THUNDER, WIND SOUNDS sneak in. HOMER ENTERS
to watch the coming storm.)

HOMER. Would you look at those thunderheads.

CRUTCH. Rollin in blacker than sin on a Sunday.

HOMER. *(Hopeful)* Well. Maybe she'll blow right on by us.

CRUTCH. I doubt it, Homer.

HOMER. I don't mind rain/but I hate that durn thunder.

CRUTCH. Aw, it's just the Good Lord up there blowin His nose. /

(THUNDER closer now, louder. WIND SOUNDS are rising.)

HOMER. I've seen some hellers in my day, but this takes the cake. /

(JUNE runs on, worried.)

JUNE. Mr. Collins, have you seen my dog?
CRUTCH. Nope.
HOMER. If that dog of yours has any smarts, it's hidin out, Juney.
JUNE. Ma claims she spotted a funnel cloud yonder!
HOMER. A twister?!
CRUTCH. It's weather for twisters, no question there.
JUNE. I gotta find my dog! /

(JUNE runs off calling for "Lady." We hear her continuing to call from off-stage as the STORM sounds grow even more intense.)

CRUTCH. You best get yourself down to the storm cellar, June!
HOMER. It's fixin to break any minute!
CRUTCH. *(Exiting)* I'm gonna head for shelter myself.
HOMER. *(Exiting)* I tell you, it's blowin in fast!

(The STORM BREAKS WIDE OPEN. THUNDER and LIGHTNING ECHO THROUGH THE THEATER. A TRAP DOOR pops open and REBEKAH pokes her head out. Note: if your stage has no trap, just enter.)

REBEKAH. June!!/Come on, honey!/
JUNE. *(Entering, upset.)* I can't find my dog!
REBEKAH. Don't you have enough sense to get out of the weather?! /

(JUNE sees something in the sky — she's awe-struck by the sight.)

JUNE. What in the world is that thing?
REBEKAH. It's a tornado, June! What do you think it is?!
JUNE. *(Points out over the audience.)* Just look at it, Ma!/
REBEKAH. *(Sees "it" now.)* Oh, my heavenly days./

(JUNE raps at another "storm cellar" as REBEKAH stares at the heavens.)

JUNE. Preacher?/ Hey, Reverend?!/ Come look at this, will you? /

(The stage begins filling with PEOPLE, faces all turned to the downstage sky. What they see is an off-stage "balloonist" caught in the storm — and nobody has ever seen anything like this before.)

REBEKAH. What in creation is that?
PHINEAS. Good God Almighty!
JUNE. I think it's a man up there!
TINY. Sweet Jesus!
REBEKAH. It is a man!
JUNE. It's him, Ma! It's him!
CRUTCH. He's blowin right for us!
TOWNSPEOPLE. —What's all the commotion about? —It's right over yonder!—He's comin!—What's comin?!

("The BALLOON," unseen by the audience, is blowing right for them. THEY all turn as one body, to follow "it.")

HOMER & PHINEAS. —Good God! —It's fixin to —

BALLOONIST'S VOICE. *(Live, shouted from above:)* Look out below!!

TOWNSPEOPLE. —He's— —He's— —He's— —Oh, my God! — Take cover, ladies!/

(A BOOT FALLS FROM THE SKY! The TOWNSPEOPLE gather around it.)

BALLOONIST'S VOICE. *(Blowing "past" them:)* Helllllloooooo down theeeeeereee!!! /

TINY. It's Jesus! He's Jesus!

BELVA. He dropped his boot.

CRUTCH & HOMER. Look out for the trees!

TINY. He's headin right for the river!

PHINEAS. The river?! /

(JUNE runs off up left, shouting:)

JUNE. I got him! I got him! /

(The TOWN watches as off-stage JUNE grabs an off-stage rope and is "lifted" high into the sky.)

REBEKAH. Juney!/Come down from there!!/

JUNE. Ahhhhhh!!!

WOMEN. Ahhhhhhhhhh!!!!

HOMER. Hang on, Juney! /

(JUNE and the BALLOONIST both fall into the off-stage "river," up left. Everyone runs off to help except TINY, who's holding the boot from above.)

MAGGIE. Oh, my God!

HOMER. *(Exiting)* Juney!!

REBEKAH. Swim, baby, swim!!

TINY. Somebody save him!

TOWNSPEOPLE. *(Exiting, and off-stage voices:)*—I'll get her!—Gangway now!—Juney?—Keep hold of my arm!—Grab him!—He's got him!—Juney?!

TINY. *(Exiting)* Don't lose him!

(The stage is empty.)

TOWNSPEOPLE.—Hold on! —We got him!—Jesus in Heaven! —Look out folks! —Make way!!

(The BALLOONIST stumbles on as if thrust onto stage. We assume he's soaking wet, but no real water or damp clothes are neces-sary. He falls to the floor, gasping for breath. The TOWNS-PEOPLE rush back on and gather around him. Note: the worst of the storm has passed, but there's still plenty of WIND and RAIN.)

TINY. Is he alright?

CRUTCH. Don't crowd him now —

PHINEAS. Give him air, people!

BALLOONIST. *(Gasping)* Where am I?

BELVA. You're in Gray, stranger!

BALLOONIST. Gray?

TINY. You want your boot back?

(Commotion upstage as REBEKAH and HOMER enter— HOMER carries a lifeless-looking JUNE in his arms. The attention shifts to JUNE.)

REBEKAH. Oh, my Lord! Oh, God!

HOMER. Pastor, come look at her!

PHINEAS. Juney?

HOMER. I don't think she's breathin.

(EVERYONE except the BALLOONIST is gathered around JUNE now.)

REBEKAH. Somebody help her!

PHINEAS. *(Patting JUNE'S hand, frantically.)* Juney, come to...!

HOMER. Breathe, Juney.

REBEKAH. *(Crying)* Oh, my God, baby.

BELVA. She's fixin to die!

BALLOONIST. *(Alone)* Is her heart beating?

REBEKAH. What?

BALLOONIST. Does she have a pulse?

REBEKAH. *(Panicked)* I don't know—I just—

CRUTCH. Give him room, people— let the man through.

REBEKAH. Juney?

BALLOONIST. Ma'am, stand back— I'll do what I can.

PHINEAS. Lord God, we ask you to heal and bless her.

(CRUTCH speaks to the audience, as the action continues:)

CRUTCH. This stranger among us — this man from the sky — knelt down beside her and took that girl's face in his hands — and then an amazing thing happened:

TINY. Sweet Jesus...

CRUTCH. He held to that child and blew his own breath in her body. And I mean to tell you, the very same moment she opened her eyes, the wind ceased to howlin and the rain stopped to fallin like that.

(CRUTCH snaps his fingers once — the rain and wind instantly stop! JUNE coughs.)

BALLOONIST. She's breathing...

TOWNSPEOPLE. —She's breathin.—She's breathin! — Praise God, she's alive!

HOMER. Was he kissin her?

CRUTCH. Oh, for the love of God, Homer.

BELVA. Say, what's your name, Mister?

BALLOONIST. Ma'am, I don't know as I quite comprehend it myself, but the fact is my name's Gray.

BELVA. Gray, you say?

TOWNSPEOPLE. —Gray? —G-R-A-Y??? —He says his name's Gray!

GRAY. *(The Balloonist.)* Galen P. Gray, Ma'am. The pleasure's all mine.

PHINEAS. If that's not the darndest thing I ever heard!

TOWNSPEOPLE. —Where do you hail from? —I mean to shake that man's hand. —It's a genuine honor. —Isn't that somethin?

CRUTCH. I tell you, he plain resurrected that child!

GRAY. Sir, let's not overstate the case, please. Resurrection and resuscitation are two entirely different kettles of fish. Now: having been somewhat involved in the past with various anatomical endeavors, I'm sure you'll understand why I'm loathe to have the term "resurrectionist" attached to my person, if not my reputation per se.

CRUTCH. No offense intended.

GRAY. None taken.

PHINEAS. What in the world was that flyin contraption?

GRAY. It's called a balloon, Mister —?

PHINEAS. Wingfield. Pastor Phineas Wingfield.

GRAY. Pastor, it holds a voluminous amount of heated and hence pressurized gaseous matter —

HOMER. What?

MAGGIE. A load of hot air, Homer.

GRAY. Precisely. It's technically known as an aerostat, Ma'am. They're really quite common in France.

(REBEKAH has been tending to JUNE, who's half-sitting-up now on the far side of the stage.)

REBEKAH. Mr. Gray, I don't know how to thank you.

HOMER. Are you alright, June?

JUNE. *(Staring at GRAY.)* I feel a little lightheaded.

GRAY. *(He examines her eyes.)* You go home and get some rest, June. Everything's gonna be fine. *(To REBEKAH.)* You might give her a dosage of hot tea and sorghum to ward off any chance of the croup, Ma'am.

(REBEKAH and TINY help JUNE off.)

REBEKAH. Hot tea you say?

GRAY. Hot tea's the ticket.

HOMER. Just take her one step at a time.

GRAY. *(Turns to the men.)* Well, I don't know about you, but I could sure do with a stiff drink.

CRUTCH. If you're drinkin, Mister, I'm buyin.

(The MEN exit toward town.)

PHINEAS. *(As he exits the other direction.)* Hard drink is the downfall of civilized man.

(MAGGIE speaks to the theater.)

MAGGIE. I don't cotton to whiskey/and I can't abide smoke/ — but unlike a lot of good Christians, I'm willin to tolerate both in the name of commerce. And so, Mr. Galen P. Gray made his way down to the Corner Cafe.

(As HOMER and CRUTCH join the narration, they enter with a stool, a chair, and empty glasses, etc. There's no need for either liquids or a table.)

CRUTCH. Which ain't quite a cafe/but more of a tavern/
HOMER. It ain't even on the durn corner.

(GRAY enters during the speech below and turns his chair around backwards, so he straddles it, facing the MEN.)

GRAY. Now diet —/
MAGGIE. He said — /
GRAY. — holds the key to constitutional fortitude, friends. It just stands to reason that what you put into your system is what will eventually work its way forth.

MAGGIE. The privy's out back, if that's what you're hintin at.

GRAY. I think my gastrointestinal tract is holding up fine for the time being, Ma'am/What are your specials this evening?

MAGGIE. Meat and potatoes.

GRAY. I'll try the beef.

MAGGIE. How do you want your beef cooked?

GRAY. Well-done, please.

MAGGIE. I like it rare myself.

GRAY. Lot of folks do.

MAGGIE. Meat doesn't taste right if there's not just a little blood runnin.

GRAY. Blacken it/please/

MAGGIE. You want that seared on the outside,/pink in the middle then?/

GRAY. Ma'am,/would you please cook the steak through and through?

MAGGIE. If that's how you want it —,

GRAY. That's how I prefer it, Ma'am./Thank you./

MAGGIE. *(Exiting)* Perfect waste of a good piece of meat.../

CRUTCH. Thank God they don't have the vote. /

(The MEN clink glasses.)

HOMER. Doc/why do you take your steak black?

GRAY. It kills all the bacterial matter.

HOMER. Bacterial matter?

GRAY. Parasites/germs,/and amoebas/that's right. Germs are like dust, see? They're everywhere.They carry diseases around like a puppy totes slippers.

CRUTCH. I don't see nary a one.

GRAY. They're microscopically small, Mr. Collins, but they are/tenacious/

HOMER. There's germs in the Corner Cafe?

GRAY. From the looks of it, I'd say a few million have set up housekeeping in this very room.

CRUTCH. Good God Almighty!

GRAY. No call to panic/Whiskey's a fine way to keep them at bay/ Serves to sterilize the system/ you understand.

HOMER. What about soda pop?

GRAY. Carbonated beverages/consumed in moderation/have actually proven to benefit the metabolism, son.

HOMER. That doesn't surprise me.

(MAGGIE enters with an empty red platter, a fork and a knife.)

MAGGIE. I hope you brought your appetite with you.

HOMER. Good Lord, if that don't smell tasty, I don't know what does.

MAGGIE. I cooked it up beautiful for him.

GRAY. Madam, I told you —

MAGGIE. Oh, now — it's barely pink, Doctor. Here. Cut it.

GRAY. I've seen cows hurt worse than this get better.

MAGGIE. It's not bloody — it's juicy. It's tasty — just taste it.

(GRAY looks like he's going to be ill.)

CRUTCH. Doctor Gray?

GRAY. If you'll excuse me, I have some rather pressing business I need to attend to...

(GRAY exits off with all the dignity he can. Beat.)

MAGGIE. Well, Good Lord.

HOMER. It don't look too germy to me.

(HOMER follows the plate off as MAGGIE exits. TOWNSPEOPLE might sing a few lines of "There is Power in the Blood" to serve as a transition. Then JUNE steps into a "narrative" LIGHT.)

JUNE. Now Galen P. Gray might have been a mite squeamish

— but havin a bonafide healer in town was a new thing for people, and I don't mind tellin you we couldn't wait to get sick.

(TINY enters from one side, and GRAY from the other. The scene becomes GRAY'S "office." He doctors in street clothes — no stethoscope, nothing.)

GRAY. What seems to ail you, Miss Wingfield?

TINY. I'm just a tad on the peaked side, Doctor.

GRAY. Peaked, you say?

TINY. Yes, sir. I've got no more pep than a dog in the sun.

GRAY. Maybe you've picked up a bit of a bug.

TINY. You know what the funny thing is? No matter how worn out I get, I can't seem to sleep. I toss, turn, up, down, pacin the floorboards all night. I guess I'm just naturally nervy. I always have been.

GRAY. Stick out your tongue and say "ahh" for me, please.

TINY. Ah.

GRAY. Ahhhhh...

TINY. Ahhhhhhhhhhhhhhhhhh...

GRAY. Tonsils look normal.

TINY. I've never been to a doctor before. I want you to know I'm enjoyin it.

GRAY. Good.

TINY. I can't help but notice you don't have a ring on your finger. I take it you must be a widower, Doc?

GRAY. Never known the privilege of marriage.

TINY. Guess what? We have somethin in common. I never been married myself.

(GRAY hands TINY a small glass jar.)

GRAY. Miss Wingfield, I want you to take this jar out to the privy, and relieve yourself in it.

TINY. *(Doesn't move.)* You want to trot that thought by me again?

GRAY. I need to examine your urine, Ma'am.

TINY. What kind of animal are you?!

GRAY. I am merely trying to ascertain the root cause of your chronic insomnia.

TINY. Oh, my God, I have insomnia?!

(BELVA, CRUTCH, and MAGGIE instantly enter as GRAY exits.)

BELVA. Tell me about it.

TINY. I've suspicioned for years I had somethin drastically wrong with me, Belva — I just didn't know what it was.

MAGGIE. Guess what I have? I have migraines.

TINY. Oh, you poor thing, you.

CRUTCH. What do you do for it?

MAGGIE. Hot compress.

BELVA. Migraines ain't nothin. Mr. Collins has — what do you call it, dear?

CRUTCH. It's a dyspeptic ulcer — dear.

BELVA. I have arthritis. It's right here in my hand.

TINY. Oh, my dear God!

BELVA. *(Dry)* It's incurable

(More TOWNSPEOPLE enter, forming sort of a chorus-line of ailments.)

TINY. Insomnia.
MAGGIE. Migraines.

BELVA. Arthritis.

CRUTCH. Ulcers.

HOMER. Rheumatism.

JUNE. Menstruation.

REBEKAH. Indigestion.

TINY. Etcetera.

JUNE. From all across the county they came —

HOMER. The lame —

(REBEKAH, CRUTCH, TINY and BELVA each exit after their lines:)

REBEKAH. The infirm —

CRUTCH. The sickly —

TINY. The peaked —

BELVA. The down in the mouth —

JUNE. People flocked to the healer like birds flock to crumbs! There was somethin wrong with you if you didn't have somethin wrong with you. /

PHINEAS. *(Entering)* I tell you, I wouldn't set foot near that man!

(LIGHTS change as JUNE, MAGGIE, and HOMER cross to PHINEAS. The scene might be the pastor's front porch.)

JUNE. Why not?

PHINEAS. Cause he's nothing but trouble/ that's why./ I may not be able to read, but I have committed the bible chapter and verse to my heart./ Now you've got your leprosy/—you've got your demon possession —/ and you've got your plagues by the score/ but there isn't one single germ in the bible. /

HOMER. Folks felt a lot better before that man came to town, Pastor. It's true.

PHINEAS. I wish he'd float to whence he came, Homer.

MAGGIE. Have you got somethin personal against him, or is it just biblical?

PHINEAS. Well, I hate to talk, Margaret.

MAGGIE. I know you do, Pastor — I hate to talk, too.

PHINEAS. But Tiny told me — my own sister told me he told her to disrobe herself! And right there in front of him, too.

JUNE. Did she do it?

PHINEAS. I'm not at liberty to say. But what kind of scoundrel'd ask a fine woman, a good Christian flower to do such a thing?! I tell you, it stinks to the core.

JUNE. Personally, I'm all in favor of nudity.

MAGGIE. June.

JUNE. When I went to see him, I took all my clothes off — every last stitch — he stripped right down to his birthday suit, too. Then we danced around a fire and sacrificed small animals and house pets till the sun came up.

PHINEAS. Juney, don't josh.

HOMER. If I had a wife or a sister or a girlfriend or...somethin, I sure as heck wouldn't let her go near him.

JUNE. I best be heading for home, Pastor.

PHINEAS. Mind yourself, Juney.

HOMER. Bye, June. I'll see you at church, I hope.

JUNE. *(Homer is boring.)* Bye, Homer.

(HOMER calls after her:)

HOMER. I'll buy you a soda pop sometime.

MAGGIE. Pastor, where's Tiny been keepin herself? She wasn't to service on Sunday nor choir practice on Wednesday.

PHINEAS. That durn doctor told her to sleep in the daytime and stay up all night.

MAGGIE. Well I never heard such a thing.

PHINEAS. Tiny told me she saw him late last night — and just take a guess where he was/ *(Dramatic beat.)* Graveyard.//

MAGGIE. The graveyard?

HOMER. What in the world was Doc doin out there?

MAGGIE. Did he have a shovel?

PHINEAS. Oh, he's some kind of secretive Free-Thinker, Maggie — there's no tellin what he could do! Dig up dead people — desecrate bodies — just for curiosity's sake.

HOMER. He wasn't diggin up dead people, is he?

PHINEAS. I don't think we've sunk to that yet. But I know a preacher who knows of a fella who talked to somebody who lives in the city —

MAGGIE. And?

PHINEAS. Apparently, there was a doctor he knew, kept a whole jar of gizzards —/ and I'm talkin human-type gizzards —/ pickled right there on his desk!

HOMER. Pickled 'em?

PHINEAS. Pickled 'em, / that's what he did! Just like a Godblessit cucumber, Homer!/ I tell you, it gives a man pause.

MAGGIE. *(Exiting:)* I don't know what this world's comin to.

(TINY enters with a length of rope as PHINEAS and MAGGIE exit.)

TINY. *(To us:)* Shhhh./ In reality, I'm sound asleep right now./ But for purposes of telling this story/ I am a tree.

HOMER. *(To us:)* I'm a tree with a swing in me./

TINY. This is a clothesline.//

HOMER. And this is June's yard. And in case you ain't

guessed it by now, I am one tree with a real bad crush on the prettiest girl in the county.

(They stretch the "clothesline" between them as REBEKAH and JUNE enter with a basket of laundry to hang on the line. Note: we don't need too many articles of clothing to get the point across.)

JUNE. Mama?

REBEKAH. Yes, June?

JUNE. Do you think you'll ever get married again?

REBEKAH. I doubt it.

JUNE. Why not?

REBEKAH. Because I'm still in love with your father, that's why. I imagine I always will be.

JUNE. But, Ma, just suppossin you met somebody you liked a lot, and he liked you back, and he asked you to marry him? What do you think you'd do then?

REBEKAH. Honey, that's not gonna happen.

JUNE. But what if it did?

REBEKAH. It won't.

JUNE. I ain't sayin it will, but it's possible, ain't it?

REBEKAH. June. What's your point?

JUNE. I think we should ask Doctor Gray over for dinner.

REBEKAH. No.

JUNE. Why not?

REBEKAH. Because I have no interest in courtin that man. None whatsoever.

JUNE. Well what if I do?

REBEKAH. Oh, Lord, June.

JUNE. I like him. I really do, Ma. I mean I really, really like him.

REBEKAH. Juney, he's too old for you.

JUNE. You were in love at my age.

REBEKAH. Yes, but your Pa was no older than me.

JUNE. I'm old enough to know how I feel.

REBEKAH. Honey, you don't even know Doctor Gray.

JUNE. Then why don't we ask him to dinner and rectify that?

REBEKAH. No, June.

JUNE. But, Ma —

REBEKAH. I said no, honey.

JUNE. *(After a moment.)* Maybe he could just make a house call or somethin.

REBEKAH. You're not sick.

JUNE. Well you are.

REBEKAH. I am not ill in the least.

JUNE. Then how come you keep throwin up in the mornin? *(Off her mother's look:)* Are you havin a baby?

REBEKAH. *(After a moment.)* I don't know.

JUNE. What do you mean you don't know?

REBEKAH. I mean I don't know if am or not yet.

JUNE. Maybe you should ask Doctor Gray.

REBEKAH. We've already spoken about it. At length.

JUNE. What did he say?

REBEKAH. I don't want to talk about this.

JUNE. You sure act like you're havin a baby.

REBEKAH. Honey, look at me. *(JUNE does.)* We don't need another mouth to feed. Right now, it's all I can do to look after you and take care of myself, honey. Do you understand what I'm tellin you?

JUNE. No.

REBEKAH. *(After a moment.)* I'll explain it sometime when you're older.

(REBEKAH exits. JUNE turns to us:)

JUNE. The first thing I'm plannin to do when I'm older is move to the city, and set up housekeepin with Galen P. Gray. He'll teach me to nurse. I'll help him with patients. And we'll live in a real nice house with a nice little office downstairs. I'll cook him nice meals, he'll buy me nice clothes, and we'll have lots of lots of children — which means we'll need to spend an inordinate amount of time in the bedroom. And that's just the way it's gonna be.

(HOMER turns to us as JUNE exits:)

HOMER. If oak trees could talk, I'd be cryin.

(Night. BELVA and CRUTCH rush on stage. BELVA carries a lantern. CRUTCH has a red rag wrapped around his hand, signifying that he's cut himself. BELVA knocks, or we hear the sound of her knocking, as:)

BELVA. Doctor Gray? Doctor, wake up!
CRUTCH. You know it's the funniest thing, Bel — it really don't hurt at'all.
BELVA. *(Knocks again.)* Doc? Are you decent?
GRAY. *(O.S.)* Be right with you, people!
CRUTCH. Sorry to wake you.

(GRAY enters, barefooted and buttoning his shirt. He's just woken up.)

GRAY. What's wrong, Mrs. Collins? You taking ill?
BELVA. It ain't me, it's him, Doc. He's cut his hand bad.

GRAY. Oh, no...

CRUTCH. I was tryin to sharpen a plow.

BELVA. I went to bed early; I went to sleep directly —

CRUTCH. I's intendin to plant by the light of the moon.

BELVA. Next thing I knew, Mr. Collins is standin there bleedin all over my clean sheets.

GRAY. *(Avoids looking at it.)* How bad is it?

CRUTCH. Well, It's a gash, Doc, there's no question there.

GRAY. How deep is it?

CRUTCH. Well look at it. Isn't that somethin? You see all them — what do you call em? — them innard things?

BELVA. Tendons, I reckon.

(GRAY passes out. Beat.)

CRUTCH. Doc?

BELVA. Good Lord, he's fell back to sleep.

CRUTCH. Honey, I don't believe he's sleepin. I think the man fainted flat out.

BELVA. I'll fetch some water — we'll bring him around.

(BELVA exits.)

CRUTCH. *(Privately)* Hey, Galen — snap to now — let's sober up, buddy.

GRAY. *(Groggy)* What...?

CRUTCH. *(Calls)* He's comin around, Belva!

(BELVA enters with a BUCKET.)

BELVA. Just hold on — I'll give him a dowsin.

GRAY. What?..ho—ho—whoa!—hold it a second! Just let

me clear my mind, will you? *(Pulling himself together.)* Mr. Collins, if you'll dip your hand in that bucket and clean it off for me, I can't tell you how much that would aid my examination...

CRUTCH. Sure, I can swush it around.

GRAY. You got a knife on you?

CRUTCH. Bel, fish it out of my pocket here for me.

BELVA. You feelin alright, Doc?

CRUTCH. *(Her hand is in his pocket.)* Watch it there, Belva.

GRAY. I'm gonna be fine, Ma'am.

(She gives him the pocket knife. GRAY cuts a strip or two off of his button-down white shirt, as they talk.)

CRUTCH. Good Lord, this water is gettin dark fast.

BELVA. Doc, how to manage to —?

GRAY. Operate, Madam? I don't. I can't do it. That's all there is to it.

BELVA. What kind of doctor can't cut on nobody?

GRAY. Dead folks I don't have much trouble with, but live ones just take the starch out of my system in two seconds flat.

BELVA. Must make it difficult for you.

GRAY. It curses me, Ma'am. It's a terrible failing, it truly is.

CRUTCH. Doc, if you want, I'll just go home and let'er stop bleedin alone.

GRAY. *(It's tempting, but...)* No! No, you might get infected, I'd hate to have that. Just hold it out here and I'll try to bind it up properly. *(To BELVA.)* Take his arm for me, please. *(GRAY can hardly bear to look at the "gash". CRUTCH'S HAND shakes a little.)* If you could steady it, Ma'am...I'm trying to put myself in a mind of cadavers.

(GRAY binds CRUTCH'S hand, as:)

CRUTCH. It's a wonder to me it don't hurt anymore than it does.

GRAY. It might be you sliced a nerve open. You feel numb?

CRUTCH. No.

GRAY. Wiggle your fingers around for me. *(CRUTCH does.)* I think you're gonna be fine. Main thing's to keep the skin grafting together.

BELVA. Doc, what is this mark on his arm? *(The mark is invisible to us.)*

GRAY. Could be a mole or a birthmark.

CRUTCH. I never noticed that, Belva.

GRAY. You got any others?

CRUTCH. Not that I know of.

BELVA. Look! There's a mark on me, too.

CRUTCH. I'll be dog gone.

GRAY. Could be some type of eczema, I suppose. Does it itch?

BELVA. No.

GRAY. Let me know if it changes shape any or gets any bigger.

CRUTCH. You tie a right handsome knot, Doc.

GRAY. Keep it dry. Keep it clean. Don't try to plow, for God's sake. You show infection the crack of a door, it barges right in like a Mormon. Good night all.

CRUTCH. I thank you again, sir. Sleep tight.

(GRAY exits.)

BELVA. I'm too young for age spots.

CRUTCH. I'd call it a beauty mark, Belva.

BELVA. A beauty mark?

CRUTCH. What do you say you and me take the long way home, honey?

BELVA. Mr. Collins, are you spoonin me?

CRUTCH. This much excitement at this time of night, just puts a man of a mood.

BELVA. I think you should hurt yourself more often.

(MUSIC. LIGHTS rise on REBEKAH, who speaks to the theater. MUSIC supports her thoughts, her speech.)

REBEKAH. In the long days that followed the death of my husband, I dreamt about him near every night. In my dreams, my husband rose up from the earth; the dust fell from his eyes; and his voice was so familiar and lonesome, it scared me. Sometimes I could feel his breath through the window. I could feel his touch in my sleep. *(Then)* And so, when I found myself dreaming in tears, and I woke up alone, I went to the graveyard to see him.

(GRAY enters the graveyard, late at NIGHT. We barely see him...more shadow than presence. He takes a yarmulke out of his pocket, puts it on, and softly begins to say Kaddish:)

GRAY. *(Half-whispering.)* "Yis-gad-dalv'yis-kad-dash sh'meh rab-bo, b'ol-mo di'v-ro kir'-u-seh v'yam-lich mal-chu-seh, b'cha-ye-chon u-'yo-me-chon u-v'cha-yeh d'chol bes yis-ro-el —"

REBEKAH. What are you sayin?

(She's startled him. He takes his yarmulke off.)

GRAY. Mrs. Muldoon...! Fancy meeting you here.

REBEKAH. What are you doin?
GRAY. I'm saying Kaddish, Ma'am.
REBEKAH. Say what?
GRAY. It's a kind of a prayer for the dead.
REBEKAH. It's a foreign language, ain't it?
GRAY. To some folks it is.
REBEKAH. It sounds beautiful. Who are you prayin for?

(GRAY crouches near the old "grave," which lies flat to the earth.)

GRAY. You see this old stone here? The name's worn away, but I noticed a star on it.

REBEKAH. Oh, nobody knows who that is. We all figured he must of passed on at Christmas. On account of the star.

GRAY. No, Ma'am, that's the Star of David. I figure whoever this is, he must be one of my people.

REBEKA. You don't mean he's kin to you?

GRAY. Not by blood.

REBEKAH. *(Softly)* Would you pray that prayer for my husband? For me?

GRAY. I'd be honored to, Mrs. Muldoon.

(They cross to where her husband was buried.)

GRAY. It's a right pretty stone, Ma'am. You've done him proud.

REBEKAH. Thank you...

GRAY. This prayer for the dead is all about life. It speaks to the glory of God, but it's said for the living, you see? It's kind of a prayer for us. You understand?

REBEKAH. You're talkin about what I asked you before.

GRAY. I'm talking about your so-called "indigestion", that's right.

REBEKAH. Dr. Gray, I haven't changed my mind any. *(Near tears, but strong.)* I loved my husband more than I know how to say, but I can't have this child without him. I just can't.

GRAY. Sometimes decisions we make in a moment of grief are decisions we come to regret. Grief does terrible things to a person's mind, Ma'am, believe me, I know.

REBEKAH. I know there's certain things you can do for a woman who wants to be rid of a baby.

GRAY. I think you should give this a little more thought and a little more time.

REBEKAH. The last thing I want to give this is time! Don't you understand that? I'm only a few months along. If you don't want to help me, I'll do it myself.

GRAY. I beg you not to do that.

REBEKAH. I've heard tell of roots and of —

GRAY. Poisons is what they are! Do you want to kill yourself right along with it? Is that what you want? To lie in some field and bleed to death?

REBEKAH. No, sir, I don't. But I need to be shed of this baby. Why won't you help me?

GRAY. *(A near-whisper.)* Because I don't know if it's right.

REBEKAH. *(Meets his eye.)* Then you take it to God in prayer, sir. And you pray for the souls of us all.

(She kneels at the grave and closes her eyes. GRAY looks at her for a moment, puts his yarmulke on, looks up, and then begins to pray, letting us feel the loss in this language...slowly at first, and then more rhythmically, until the prayer becomes like a song.)

GRAY. "Yis-gad-dal v'yis-kad-dash sh'meh rab-bo, b'ol-mo di'v-ro kir'u-seh v'yam-lich mal-chu-seh, b'cha-ye-chon u-'yo-me-chon u-v'cha-yeh d'chol bes yis-ro- el, ba-a-go-lo u-viz-man ko-riv, v'im-ru O-Men. Y'heh sh'meh rab-bo m'vo-rach, l'o-lam ul'ol'meh ol-ma-ya: Yis-bo-rcah v'yish-tab-bach v'yis-po-ar, v'yis-ro-mam, v'yis-nas-seh, v'yis-had-or, v'yis-al-leh, v'yis-hal-lol O-men..."

(GRAY takes a breath at the end of this phrase, and REBEKAH, assuming he's done because it feels like he is, says:)

REBEKAH. Amen. *(He looks at her.)* I thank you.
GRAY. Mrs. Muldoon, I think that someday somebody's gonna come along, Ma'am, and see you for the good person you are. And he'll love this child, whoever he is, because it's a part of you. *(He puts his hand first on her heart, then on her womb, and then on the grave...using a line for each:)* Life is here. Life is here. Life is here.
REBEKAH. I just asked you to pray, not to preach.
GRAY. Point taken.

(They both stand.)

GRAY. Would it be too terribly forward of me to ask to escort you home, Ma'am?
REBEKAH. I don't think that'd be too awfully terrible, no.

(She takes his arm and they exit. MUSIC might be nice under the following NARRATION:)

MAGGIE. The weather report is as follows:

CRUTCH. Spring turns to Summer and Summer to Fall.

MAGGIE. There's more leaves upon the earth now than stars in the sky.

CRUTCH. And harvest is in the works.

HOMER. Sunrise'll find half the countryside out in the fields.

CRUTCH. They're shellin up corn now —

HOMER. Thrashin the wheat like a misbehaved child.

MAGGIE. But here at the preacher's house, nobody's tendin the fields this day.

CRUTCH. For here at the preacher's house, sickness has found a home.

(PHINEAS enters, sinks to a chair, and groans softly in pain as TINY lets GRAY in the "door".)

PHINEAS. Ohhhhhhhhh, my Lord...

GRAY. Morning, Miss Wingfield.

TINY. Come right in, Doctor.

PHINEAS. What is he doin here?

TINY. I sent for him, brother.

PHINEAS. *(Still doubled half-over in pain.)* Well, send him away. I don't need no doctorin.

GRAY. Pastor, you're red as a beet.

PHINEAS. *(Masking his pain.)* I'm fine — I'll be fine, thank you very much. Prayer is the answer.

TINY. Phineas, whatever this is, you can't pray it away.

PHINEAS. It passes in time every time. I appreciate your concern, sir — now why don't you show him the door?

GRAY. Why don't you tell me what's ailing you, Pastor?

TINY. Pain is what's ailin him.

GRAY. Pain in the abdomen?

PHINEAS. *(Groans, sounds like "lower")* Looooord...

GRAY. Lower abdomen?

TINY. *(In confidence.)* Doctor, it's lower than lower.

GRAY. Miss Tiny, could we have a moment of privacy, please?

TINY. But, Doc —

GRAY. *(Walks her out of the room.)* You just wait out in the hall. He'll be fine. You sleeping alright, are you?

TINY. I love the night.

GRAY. Good!

TINY. I'll pray for you, brother.

(TINY exits. GRAY turns back and matter-of-factly announces:)

GRAY. Alright, Mr. Wingfield — drop your drawers, please.

PHINEAS. Never.

GRAY. Come on now. Get out of those trousers.

PHINEAS. Get out of your own trousers!

GRAY. Let's try to be reasonable, shall we?

PHINEAS. I'm not about to slip down to my skivvies in front of the likes of you.

GRAY. Pastor —

PHINEAS. I'm not even kin to you!

GRAY. I can no more examine a patient who's fully clothed, than you'd read the bible blindfolded.

PHINEAS. I know my scriptures.

GRAY. *(Stares at him, then.)* Alright, to heck with you.

(GRAY drops his own trousers.)

PHINEAS. What are you doin?

GRAY. If I can do it, you can do it. Come on, sir. Drop your pants.

PHINEAS. *(Averts his eyes.)* "Blessed is he that walketh not in the counsel of the ungodly, nor standeth in the way of the scornful—"

(GRAY joins in — he knows the psalm, too. PHINEAS looks up, amazed. After a moment, the preacher drops his own trousers as they recite the psalm together. Both men end up with their pants around their ankles.)

GRAY. *(Overlapping.)*	PHINEAS. *(Overlapping.)*
"—But his delight is the law of the Lord. And he shall be like a tree planted by the rivers of water, that bringeth forth fruit in his season—"	"—But his delight is the law of the Lord. And he shall be like a tree planted by the rivers of water, that bringeth forth fruit in his season"

GRAY. Etcetera, etcetera, and so on.

PHINEAS. Amen.

GRAY. Now: let's see if we can get to the bottom of this, so to speak.

PHINEAS. Don't touch me.

GRAY. I know you're tender.

PHINEAS. Just keep your paws to yourself!

(GRAY and PHINEAS mirror each other, so that GRAY examines his own body.)

GRAY. *(Touching his own belly.)* Would you say the pain is localized about here?

PHINEAS. A tad lower.

GRAY. Here?

PHINEAS. South, and a tad to the East.

GRAY. So it's in the region of the groin, if you'll pardon my French?

PHINEAS. It feels like somebody stuck a knife in me.

GRAY. Sharp pain or dull?

PHINEAS. Shootin clean through to my backside.

GRAY. And does your urine have a...darkish hue to it?

PHINEAS. It's bloody as all get out, yeah.

(GRAY sits down to think. Starts to cross his legs, discovers he can't — then continues his diagnosis in a business-like fashion.)

GRAY. Mr. Wingfield, I believe you've got a stone, sir.

PHINEAS. A stone?

GRAY. A kidney stone, likely. It blocks the urethra, causes some swelling, a great deal of discomfort.

PHINEAS. Are you gonna cut on me?

GRAY. Pastor, I'd hope to avoid that, I truly would. First thing to do is to try and relieve the pain.

PHINEAS. Doc, I'd be more than grateful.

GRAY. You know Benjamin Franklin, my personal favorite among the Founding Fathers, suffered from the very same ailment.

PHINEAS. Ben Franklin had stones?

GRAY. Oh, he had a stone the size of Gibraltar. He was plagued with such pain, it just about crippled him. But being a man of some scientific prowess, he relieved himself of it by reversing the gravitational flow, inverting the torso — thereby releasing his stone from the groinular region.

PHINEAS. Meanin?

GRAY. He stood on his head.

PHINEAS. *(Starts to cross away.)* You got another think comin.

GRAY. The pain will get worse. Your plumbing backs up, septicemia sets in, and the body begins to poison itself.

(PHINEAS stops. GRAY has his attention.)

GRAY. That stone's lodged as tight as a drum in your tract. But merely invert the torsonic position, put physics to work — and that thing will rise up and free itself, Pastor.

PHINEAS. *(Reluctantly)* Well...if it worked for Ben Franklin — him bein a Founder and all...

GRAY. Turn around, sir. That's it. Crouch down, put your hands on the floor.

(PHINEAS crouches. GRAY is right behind him. Both men's pants are around their ankles. PHINEAS glances back, worried.)

GRAY. Trust me.

PHINEAS. I'm tryin.

GRAY. Upsy daisy now...here we go!

(GRAY takes PHINEAS' legs and thrusts them in the air, so the pastor stands on his head. PHINEAS screams. TINY rushes in.)

PHINEAS. OHHHHHHHHHHH GOD!!!

TINY. Phineas! Brother, are you alright?!

PHINEAS. Jesus in heaven!

GRAY. Miss Tiny—please! Madam, avert your eyes!

TINY. What in the world are you doin to him?
(GRAY tries to pull his trousers up with one hand while holding
PHINEAS up with the other — it isn't easy.)

PHINEAS. Whoaaaaa!!!
GRAY. If you'd allow us a modicum of modesty, Ma'am—
PHINEAS. Praise God!! I've been healed!!
TINY. You're healed?!
PHINEAS. Oh, blessed relief!!
TINY. *(To GRAY.)* What are your pants doin down?
GRAY. It's all in the interest of science, Miss Tiny. If you'll
just give me a hand with his...what is this mark on your leg?!

(GRAY notices a "mark" on the pastor's calf — like BELVA'S and
CRUTCH'S.)

PHINEAS. Oh, God, I haven't felt this good in ages.
GRAY. Pastor, have you ever scrutinized this?
TINY. I've noticed the same things on me. I got one up here,
and another right chere, on back of my drum stick.
GRAY. Tiny, if you'll take his feet for a second—
TINY. Surely.
GRAY. —I'd like to examine that.
PHINEAS. *(As TINY takes solo leg duty.)* Watch it now—
GRAY. Just keep his toes to the heavens, Ma'am. Keep breath-
ing, Pastor. You doing alright?
PHINEAS. Tiny, this man's an unqualified genius.
GRAY. I hope you don't mind if I—
TINY. Hike it on up there and you take a gander.

(GRAY lifts TINY'S skirts up, and examines the back of her thigh.)

PHINEAS. How long you figure I oughta do this?

GRAY. Sooner or later that stone's gonna have to come out. Let's just hope it passes of its own accord, sir.

TINY. See? It ain't bruised, is it?

GRAY. No, Ma'am, it's clearly a mark of some sort.

PHINEAS. Doc, I'm startin to get a mite dizzy here.

GRAY. Alright, let's let him down. *(Helping TINY lower him.)* Easy now. There we go.

PHINEAS. *(Lying on the ground.)* Lord.

GRAY. I warn you: the pain's gonna strike again, sir. They say the only thing worse than passing a kidney stone's birthing a baby. Just rise up a tad at a time.

TINY. Leastways he knows what to do for it now.

PHINEAS. Doctor, we surely give thanks.

GRAY. Pastor. Miss Tiny.

(REBEKAH enters and GRAY crosses as:)

REBEKAH. Of course I don't have any marks on my person.

PHINEAS. *(Exiting with his sister.)* Tiny, I've misjudged him.

(REBEKAH is seven or eight months pregnant now, and definitely "showing". The bench from the preacher's house will soon become a "boat". There's a "paddle" built into the side of it, disguised as a cross beam or support. Or else a platform becomes a "boat" or a "raft".)

GRAY. Just next time you bathe yourself, Becky, be sure to look yourself over.

REBEKAH. I never come down with a thing when I'm pregnant. I can't even catch a cold.

GRAY. *(Helping her into the "boat".)* That's just an old wives tale.

REBEKAH. Well, I'm an old wife, and I believe it. Be careful, Galen. This old johnny boat's always been tippy. Sit down. Sit down. Sit, sit, sit for Pete's sake!

GRAY. I'm not completely incompetent in matters of physical prowess. I've captained a balloon for God's sake.

REBEKAH. You're facin the wrong direction, Captain.

GRAY. So I am.

(He turns around so they're facing each other.)

REBEKAH. Mind your balance now.

GRAY. There. That's a little more like it.

(He paddles the "boat" away from the shore, the stage floor is lit with a BLUE/GREEN wash, and they're out on the river...)

GRAY. Bid farewell to civilization, such as it is.

REBEKAH. Adam and I used to picnic on up in that cove over yonder.

GRAY. I'll paddle you somewhere else then.

REBEKAH. *(After a moment.)* Don't get us caught in the current now.

(He paddles for a moment or two; she relaxes, taking in the view...)

REBEKAH. Gosh, it's a lovely day, ain't it?

GRAY. Becky, I've travelled from here to the edge of the sea itself, but I've got to honestly tell you, the scenery I'm taking in right here and now is just about as scenic as scenery can be.

REBEKAH. You mean up in your balloon?

GRAY. The balloon was an interesting means of transportation at an extraordinarily inopportune time, but I think I'd just as soon stay a little closer to home from now on.

REBEKAH. Is this home to you now?

GRAY. Home's always been people, not places for me. My pa was a travelling medicine man, you see.

REBEKAH. You mean a doctor like you?

GRAY. No, I mean he was a charlatan, Becky. We used to sell remedies out of the back of a wagon.

REBEKAH. You didn't?

GRAY. Nostrum's Elixer & Medical Cure-All, yes, Ma'am. "A recuperative miracle," Pa used to call it. Oh, he could sell dog shit to cats, that man could.

REBEKAH. What's it do to you?

GRAY. Well, you funnel a mixture of alcohol, prune juice, and cod's liver oil down any man's gullet, it moves him in more ways than one.

REBEKAH. *(Touches her stomach.)* Oh, good heavens...

GRAY. What?

REBEKAH. I feel it. Right here. It's kickin.

GRAY. *(Pleased)* Well isn't something? I wonder if I could hear his heart yet? You don't mind, do you?

REBEKAH. Galen! You're rockin the boat.

GRAY. I'm not gonna capsize us, Becky.

REBEKAH. Be careful.

GRAY. Good golly, you are a worry wart. *(He places his head on her womb:)* Interesting...interesting.

REBEKAH. What do you hear?

GRAY. Hello in there!

REBEKAH. Galen!

GRAY. Hold on — he's tapping out a message. *(Listens)* He

wants to know what his name is.

REBEKAH. If it's a boy you can tell him I've settled on Galen.

GRAY. *(Looks up, perplexed, disturbed.)* Don't get me wrong here — I feel a foot taller, Becky, I do — but a name is a holy thing. A good name should honor an ancestor. I'd name a son for his father.

REBEKAH. It isn't his child. (GRAY takes this in for a moment.) It isn't mine neither. It's yours, Doctor Gray.

GRAY. Mine, Ma'am?

REBEKAH. You're the one havin this baby, not me. You wanted it, Galen — you got it.

GRAY. Now, Becky —

REBEKAH. I done made my mind up — after I birth him, I'll give him to you.

GRAY. That's a mighty sweet thought, it truly is —

REBEKAH. It ain't a thought, sir: it's a fact.

GRAY. Becky, now —

REBEKAH. I think you'll make a fine mother.

GRAY. Becky, I can't raise a child alone!

REBEKAH. Well somebody has to!

(We hear JUNE calling in the distance:)

JUNE. Doctor Gray—? Doctor—?

(REBEKAH has the paddle now. She starts for "shore".)

REBEKAH. We better head for shore, Galen.

GRAY. Diapers and feeding and — Jesus Jehova!

JUNE. *(Closer now.)* Hey, Doctor—?

REBEKAH. *(Calls)* He's over here, June!

GRAY. Alright, alright you've made your point, Becky, I've had my comeupance — now let's quit this funning around, shall we?

REBEKAH. Galen: this baby belongs to you.

GRAY. *(Realizes she fully means it.)* Oh, my dear God.

(JUNE appears on the horizon. As REBEKAH rows them closer to "shore," the RIVER LIGHT RECEDES...)

JUNE. Doc, I been lookin all over for you!

GRAY. Juney, just hold on a second! *(To BECKY.)* If you want a ring on your finger, there's better ways, Becky.

REBEKAH. Don't flatter yourself.

JUNE. Doc, you need to run to the Collins house — right away.

REBEKAH. Juney, what's wrong, honey?

JUNE. Belva's been coughin just awful. She's runnin a fever — she can't hardly breathe!

REBEKAH. Oh, my lord. *(To GRAY.)* Is there anything I can do?

GRAY. Oh, I think you've accomplished enough for one day.

(REBEKAH exits as LIGHTS rise on BELVA COUGHING — it's a terrible, deep, soul-wracking cough. She draws long, raspy, labored breaths. CRUTCH helps her on stage.)

JUNE. You want me to stay on and help you? Cause I've always been interested in nursin and whatnot.

GRAY. Mrs. Collins?

CRUTCH. Doctor Gray's here now — he'll tend to you,

honey.

GRAY. Bring me a basin of boiling hot water.

JUNE. What do you think's wrong with her?

GRAY. Now, Juney.

CRUTCH. Do what he tells you, girl.

(JUNE rushes off stage. BELVA COUGHS deeply. The cough is so intense that it brings her to her knees.)

GRAY. Easy now...easy, Ma'am...just let it pass.

CRUTCH. God, I don't know what this is.

(BELVA takes her hand away from her mouth; she has a small RED HANDKERCHIEF, signifying that she's just coughed up BLOOD...)

CRUTCH. Belva?

GRAY. Dear God Almighty.

CRUTCH. Doctor Gray?

GRAY. Easy now, easy...just take it one breath at a time.

(GRAY turns away, struggling to keep it "together.")

CRUTCH. Doctor?

GRAY. *(Still away.)* Don't let the blood frighten you, Ma'am...there is absolutely nothing to be afraid of. You're gonna be just fine, just fine...just breathe right on past it and think about something else.

CRUTCH. Don't tell me you're weak in the knees again. You need a drink?

GRAY. *(He gives CRUTCH his handkerchief.)* Just clean her up a bit for me. *(To himself.)* You just need to slow down and concentrate. Slow down and breathe.

    CRUTCH. Good lord, you scared me to death, honey.

(CRUTCH wipes the "blood" from his wife's mouth and hand. BELVA'S BREATHING sounds almost like an asthma attack — as if each new breath were a struggle. GRAY places his head on her back or chest — he almost steadies himself with his patient.)

    GRAY. Alright...alright...we're gonna get through this, I promise. I want you to take a good breath for me, Belva. That's it... breathe deep as you can now, and hold it, please. Hold it.

    CRUTCH. It seems like choking inside her own body.

(JUNE enters with a STEAMING BASIN of "water" and a large enough towel or cloth to cover BELVA'S head and upper body.)

    JUNE. Dr. Gray?

    GRAY. Bring it right here.

    JUNE. What's wrong with her?

    CRUTCH. She's been coughin up blood, Juney.

    JUNE. Blood?

    GRAY. Alright, turn your face to the light for me, Belva, and let's have a look at that throat. Open wide for me and take a deep breath. Juney, keep out of the way.

    CRUTCH. Yesterday evenin them marks of hers started to seep like a sieve. Then she set into coughin.

(SOUND OF DISTANT THUNDER...GRAY makes a sort of VAPORIZER for BELVA with the steaming basin and cloth.)

GRAY. I'm gonna cover your head with this, Ma'am, and I want you to breathe in some steam. There we go, Belva. There you go... That feels a mite better, I'd think.

CRUTCH. Doctor, d'ja hear me?

GRAY. I heard, sir.

JUNE. It's fixin to rain.

(JUNE is with BELVA. GRAY and CRUTCH step away for privacy.)

GRAY. Last night her marks started to seep, you say?

CRUTCH. Puffed up the size of a damn silver dollar and blistered wide open.

GRAY. Whatever these lesions are, I think they've cropped up and festered inside her. They've spread to her throat, and her lungs. Do you understand what I'm saying to you?

CRUTCH. You're saying I'm gonna come down with this, too.

(It begins to RAIN...not a storm, but a steady rain.)

GRAY. Mr. Collins: I want this house quarantined.

CRUTCH. Quarantine?

JUNE. *(Looking up at the weather.)* Good lord, it's comin down fast.

CRUTCH. Why has God done this to her?

(GRAY crosses back to BELVA, whose breathing is labored. For a good moment, all we hear is her struggle for breath and the RAIN...and then JUNE steps downstage.)

JUNE. And so ends chapter one.

(THUNDER CRASHES. LIGHTS TO BLACK.)

ACT II

(LIGHTS RISE on several TOWNSPEOPLE. They speak to the theater.)

MAGGIE. The weather report is as follows:
PHINEAS. There was thunder —
TINY. And lightning —
PHINEAS. And sickness —
TINY. And dread.
MAGGIE. Everyday somebody found a mark on em.
TINY. Every night somebody else took a fever.
PHINEAS. And still, it continued to spread.
JUNE. Anatomy of Gray.
TOWNSPEOPLE. Chapter Two:

(Lights isolate JUNE.)

JUNE. This time — this terrible onslaught of sickness — was a frightening time; but secretly, for a girl who was fated to live in the most boring town in the world — secretly it was also the best of times — because she got to spend so much time with Doctor Galen P. Gray. In fact, the doctor and June were together so much, one would think they were practically married. Except for the fact

they didn't have sex or sleep in the same bed or kiss or hold hands
— there was very little that they did not share. She went where he
went; she did what he did. For June had become his assistant.

*(GRAY enters feeling faint, gasping for air. He ends up next to
JUNE.)*

GRAY. Oh, God, oh, God...

*(He puts his hands on his knees. JUNE waves her hand in his face.
It's obvious they've been through this before.)*

JUNE. Just take it one breath at a time, Doc, you're gonna be
fine. Drink?

(GRAY pulls a small flask from his jacket. Takes a sip.)

GRAY. Thank you.
JUNE. Why are you so scared of blood?
GRAY. I don't know.
JUNE. You think you'll ever get over it?
GRAY. Do we have to talk about this?
JUNE. Why do you wash your hands after every single
patient?
GRAY. Because it stops the spread of germs.
JUNE. How?
GRAY. I don't know, it just does.
JUNE. Well if washin kills germs, then why don't you make
everybody who's marked take a bath and just wash the marks off
em?
GRAY. Because it doesn't work that way, June.

JUNE. Why not?

GRAY. Because the marks are an external symptom of an illness that's already inside them, that's why.

JUNE. Then why don't you wash out their innards? Make em drink soap and hot water to kill the germs.

GRAY. That wouldn't work.

JUNE. Why not?

GRAY. Because the sickness has already taken root in the bloodstream and spread through their systems.

JUNE. Is that why you're scared of blood?

GRAY. Can I ask you a question? Why do you ask so many questions?

JUNE. Because you told me there's no such thing as a dumb question, only a dumb answer.

GRAY. Well I love your questions.

JUNE. You do?

GRAY. In fact, I love them so much I want to parcel them out. From now on, I want you to limit yourself to one question a day.

JUNE. One a day?

GRAY. One a day.

(TOWNSPEOPLE narrate the Q & A for us; they're fairly formal about it.)

REBEKAH. Monday:

JUNE. Do you believe in God?

GRAY. Yes.

REBEKAH & TINY. Tuesday:

JUNE. Do you believe God is good?

GRAY. *(After a beat.)* Yes.

REBEKAH, TINY, & HOMER. Wednesday:

JUNE. Why?

GRAY. Why what?

JUNE. Why do you believe God is good?

GRAY. Well don't you?

JUNE. I don't know. *(Off GRAY'S look.)* They say His eye is on the sparrow, but if that's true, then why do people get sick and die? I mean sparrows don't pray. They don't go to church. They don't tithe. They don't do anything but fly around and be sparrows, and if God cares more about them than he does about us, then what good is He?

GRAY. How do you know sparrows don't pray?

REBEKAH, TINY, HOMER & PHINEAS. Thursday:

JUNE. How come you've never been married?

FIVE TOWNSPEOPLE. Friday:

JUNE. Have you ever had a girlfriend?

GRAY. Yes.

JUNE. Is there anything else you want to say about that?

GRAY. No.

JUNE. *(To us:)* I wanted to ask him what happened to her — if she died tragically or flung herself from a bridge because he forsook her, or if she forsook him and left him heart-broken, and that's why he couldn't settle down and probably never would settle down til he met the right person, and I thought we both had a pretty good idea who that might be, but then, I was partly afraid the right person might be my own mother, and I couldn't bear to ask about that. Besides which, I'd already used up my question for Friday.

REBEKAH. Which brings us to —

SIX TOWNSPEOPLE. Saturday:

JUNE. Doc? What happens after we die?

GRAY. I don't know.

JUNE. Can I take back that question and ask a new question?

GRAY. Yes.

JUNE. If you believe God is good, then do you believe in heaven? And if you do, do you think I'll see my father again? And if I do, how old do you reckon I'll be when I see him? Cause I'm plannin to live as long as I can, so I'll be a lot older than him when I die, and that'll be weird cause I'll look like his mother, but feel like his daughter, except by then, I'll probably have kids of my own, and they'd get confused if I ended up younger than them — so how do you think all that sorts itself out?

GRAY. I think you'll always be your Pa's daughter, no matter how old you are.

JUNE. You think I'll ever stop missin him?

GRAY. No. I think you'll miss him for the rest of your life.

JUNE. I don't need eternity. I'd give anything just to spend a day with him. Or an afternoon even. If I could spend one afternoon with my father, that would be heaven enough for me.

GRAY. And what would you say to him, June?

JUNE. *(Close to tears or in them.)* I don't know. I guess I'd just tell him I love him, and want him back.

(He puts his hand on her shoulder.)

REBEKAH. June, bein June, saved her last, deepest, and most personal question for—

ALL TOWNSPEOPLE. Sunday.

REBEKAH. And once again, she wrote her thoughts down.

(JUNE gives GRAY a piece of paper or an envelope, which he opens and reads:)

GRAY. "Do you think I'm pretty? Check this box for 'yes' or

this box for 'no'."

REBEKAH. Oh, June.

JUNE. It may be trite and immature to you, Mother, but there's some things you don't ask out loud.

GRAY. *(Hands her the paper back.)* Juney, I think you're fifteen.

JUNE. What is that supposed to mean?

GRAY. It means I'm not gonna answer that question. Now, if you don't mind, I have patients to tend to.

(MAGGIE enters. JUNE, of course, feels slapped in the face.)

MAGGIE. Doc, I know you're busy as a three-legged cat in a sandbox, so I won't take up much of your time, but I woke up this mornin, my head hurts so badly I can't barely see.

GRAY. Do you have any fever? Aches and pains?

MAGGIE. No.

GRAY. Are your glands swollen?

MAGGIE. No, I don't think so.

(MAGGIE takes a seat, GRAY checks the glands in her neck.)

GRAY. June, will you fix a hot compress, please?

JUNE. No.

MAGGIE. Oh, I've practically soaked my durn head in hot water — it ain't helpin any. It's probably just what you said, Doc, it's probably just worry is all. *(To JUNE.)* You comin to choir tonight?

JUNE. Not if I can help it.

GRAY. Maggie: I found a mark on you.

MAGGIE. Where?

GRAY. On the back of your neck.

MAGGIE. *(A worried smile.)* I can't be marked — I haven't done anything wrong.

JUNE. Well neither has anyone else.

MAGGIE. Preacher's too prideful. Belva's a gossip. Crutch drinks like a fish. I read the bible — I pray everyday.

GRAY. If God sent down lightning to strike everybody who misbehaved, we'd have theologians predicting the weather.

MAGGIE. Well you tell me what's causin it then!

GRAY. It's a disease — it's spread by germs, not by God!

MAGGIE. I never heard of these germs things before you came here.

GRAY. Maggie, germs have been here since the dawn of creation.

MAGGIE. You're the one causin this, ain'tcha?

GRAY. Don't be ridiculous.

MAGGIE. I didn't have this before you touched me.

GRAY. Yes, you did, Maggie.

MAGGIE. *(Backing away from him.)* No, I didn't — I couldn't — I know it!

(MAGGIE exits.)

GRAY. Maggie?! Maggie, come back here! *(Turns to JUNE, frustrated.)* Would you go talk sense to that woman? Maybe she'll listen to you.

JUNE. Why would she listen to me? I'm just a kid.

(Lights bring us to evening "choir practice". TINY, REBEKAH, HOMER, and PHINEAS. MAGGIE is the choir director.)

HOMER. *(Soda pop in hand.)* Hey, June, aren't you goin to choir?

JUNE. *(Exiting)* No.

CHOIR. *(Singing this hymn or another)*
"A mighty fortress is our God,
A bulwark never failing;
Our helper he amid the flood of mortal ills
     prevailing:
For still our ancient foe doth seek to work us
     woe;
His craft and power are great,
And armed with cruel hate,
On earth is not his equal."

MAGGIE. *(Crossing away before the verse ends.)* I can't do this. I just can't go on like this as if nothin's happened at all. I can't concentrate, and I don't know how any of you can.

PHINEAS. Now, Margaret —

MAGGIE. *(Touching her "mark".)* I'm tellin you, somethin is terrible, terribly wrong with that man.

REBEKAH. Oh, now, Doctor Gray's done a world of good here. You know that as well as I do.

MAGGIE. You call bringin sickness upon us a good thing to do?

TINY. He surely did wonders for me.

MAGGIE. He's got the poor Collins locked up in their own house.

REBEKAH. That's because he's trying to keep the rest of us from catching it.

MAGGIE. Well guess what? It ain't workin.

PHINEAS. If you think this through in a factual fashion —

MAGGIE. You want the facts, Preacher? I'll give you the facts. Fact one: he touched me. Fact two: he marked me. And fact three: it's happened to you and you and now me and you know it.

HOMER. I don't have any marks on me, Maggie.

MAGGIE. You had any truck with the doctor?

HOMER. I talk to him, sure.

MAGGIE. Did he touch you?

HOMER. Well now that you mention it...

MAGGIE. Did he or didn't he?

HOMER. No.

MAGGIE. You see there?

TINY. I went to see him not two days ago.

MAGGIE. And?

HOMER. Did he touch you?

TINY. He examined me head to toe, Homer, and I'll tell you what else — if I felt any better right now, I'd be twins.

MAGGIE. Oh, why don't you go back to sleep for a couple of years?

TINY. Why don't you wake up, Maggie?

MAGGIE. You are so smitten with him you've gone blind! And you, too!

REBEKAH. Would I let my daughter near him if I thought he was causin this?

PHINEAS. Ladies — ladies! — sisters, please! *(He has their attention.)* Sickness is a hard thing to fathom, I grant. But I believe the Lord God is a loving creator. I figure the Good lord has put this mark on us to test us, don't you see?

HOMER. Test us how, Pastor?

PHINEAS. It happens right and left in the scriptures. All the saints suffer. Think about Shadrach, Meshach, and Abednego — look at how God tested Jonah and Job.

MAGGIE. Then why don't He mark Doctor Gray? He's a Jew. They claim to be God's chosen people.

TINY. Oh, everybody claims to be God's chosen people.

PHINEAS. The Jews are a bible totin people, course they only tote half of it. When the Rapture comes, I doubt your Jews'll be going to heaven. Maybe God don't want to waste His time on him.

REBEKAH. That's about the most small-minded thing I've ever heard.

HOMER. There's a mark on you, Rebekah.

REBEKAH. Oh, there is not.

PHINEAS. Where?

MAGGIE. There's a mark on her?

REBEKAH. Where?

HOMER. *(Touches his own face.)* It's right there.

MAGGIE. I don't know how he does it, but somehow he does it.

PHINEAS. Well, I've always been somewhat suspicious of him.

(CRUTCH enters.)

CRUTCH. Pastor?

MAGGIE. *(To REBEKAH.)* I'd keep your daughter away from him.

CRUTCH. Pastor?

PHINEAS. What is it? What's wrong, Mr. Collins?

CRUTCH. It's Belva. She's gone from us...

TINY. Belva? Dead?

MAGGIE. Oh, my lands.

CRUTCH. You've gotta have a strong talk with that doctor — he won't let me bury her.

PHINEAS. What do you mean?

CRUTCH. I mean he's wantin to carve on her, sir.

HOMER. Carve on a dead woman!

PHINEAS. We'll put a stop to this, Crutch — don't you worry.

HOMER. I'll come with you, Pastor.

CRUTCH. I tell ya, the man's in a frenzy.

REBEKAH. Dear Lord.

MAGGIE. *(Following the men.)* I knew it, I told you!

TINY. *(To the theatre.)* The news spread like a fire that night. A fire that was fueled by rumors, by fear, and by the fact that now even Rebekah was marked. Rebekah with child was marked. If she could be marked, then anyone could. First Juney Muldoon lost her father, now her mother was marked, and soon, she feared, soon she would be left with no one. Her boring little town wasn't boring anymore, it was dying, and it was raging, and boiling with fear. Men raced with lanterns and guns through the countryside looking for the cause of this illness: The man from the sky. The Jew. The teacher. The coward. The healer. The spreader of germs and the locus of fears: Dr. Galen Gray.

(NIGHT SOUNDS...we hear DOGS BARKING and HOWLING in the distance. And then, the sound of HORSES — not galloping, but NEIGHING, and stomping softly in the darkness as the scene becomes the "livery stable." GRAY enters quietly, deeply worried, in a hurry. He's wearing a jacket; he carries a halter. He might have a carpet bag slung over his shoulder. He doesn't see JUNE in the shadows.)

JUNE. Are you runnin away again?

GRAY. June, Is that you?

JUNE. Doc, I wouldn't do that if I was you.

GRAY. Wouldn't do what?

JUNE. I might skip town, but I sure wouldn't steal a horse. If Crutch Collins finds out you not only killed his wife, but went and took his best stallion, they'll hang you for sure.

GRAY. I didn't kill Belva — that's crazy talk.

JUNE. It may be crazy, but that's what they're sayin.

GRAY. What do you recommend I do?

JUNE. Take me along with you.

GRAY. No.

JUNE. Why not?

GRAY. Because!

JUNE. Because why? Are you mad at me?

GRAY. No, I'm not mad at you.

JUNE. I'm sorry I didn't stand up for you when you found a mark on Maggie. And I'm sorry I was fishin for compliments with that stupid check here for yes and check here for no thing — and I'm sorry I ask so many dumb questions — now will you please take me with you??

GRAY. No!

JUNE. Is it because I'm not Jewish?

GRAY. Oh, for God's sake.

JUNE. Because I can turn Jewish. I think I've always felt Jewish. I just never had a name for it before. But I'm like you. I look like everyone around here on the outside, but on the inside I've always known I was different.

GRAY. June, take my word for it: you don't need to convert just because you're an oddball.

JUNE. See? Even you think so!! Doc, I can't live here the rest of my life. I belong in the city. I want to go to museums and libraries and temples and whatnot. Gray is just...flat. Everywhere you look, it's flat. Even the hills are flat.

GRAY. Let me make this as clear as I can: you're not going with me, you're only fifteen—

JUNE. Sixteen in March.

GRAY. Your Ma's having a baby — she needs you.

JUNE. Well she needs you, too.

GRAY. Juney, my future is feathers and tar. Now I have to go.

JUNE. Will you just answer one more question before you run off? Just one more, that's all.

GRAY. What??

JUNE. Is everybody who's marked gonna die?

GRAY. I don't know. But I fear they will. You're not marked, are you?

JUNE. No. But my mother is.

HOMER. Shhhhhh!!!

GRAY. *(Reacting to the news.)* Oh, no. Oh, God...

JUNE. Does that mean her baby's marked, too?

GRAY. Shhhhh.

(HOMER has a lantern; PHINEAS brandishes a small pistol, which he isn't used to using. They enter.)

PHINEAS. My, my, my, my.

HOMER. I toldja he's down to the livery stable.

PHINEAS. Just hold it right there, Doctor Gray.

HOMER. June, has he harmed you?

JUNE. My virtue's intact, Homer, thank you for askin.

PHINEAS. Go fetch Mr. Collins, and tell him to bring a rope, son.

(HOMER exits.)

GRAY. You don't want my soul on your conscience.

JUNE. For the love of God, Pastor, you're not gonna hang him.

PHINEAS. Did you know he tried to carve poor Mrs. Collins into little tiny pieces right after she died?

GRAY. I just wanted to do an autopsy on her, that's all.

JUNE. What's an autopsy?

GRAY. June, this really isn't the best time for questions.

PHINEAS. It's the devil's work, that's what it is.

GRAY. It's an examination of the internal organs to determine the course of disease and the cause of death, sir — which wasn't me.

JUNE. Are you alright, Pastor? You look kinda flushed.

PHINEAS. It's been a long night.

(PHINEAS indeed, looks a bit pale, and his kidneys have seen better days.)

JUNE. Doc, you're not makin him sick, are you?

PHINEAS. What?

JUNE. All he has to do is just look at you cross-eyed, and boom — it's the mark of the beast.

PHINEAS. Juney: don't josh.

JUNE. He's the devil and I'm in league with him!!

GRAY. I really wish you hadn't said that.

(PHINEAS sort of backs away, and begins praying a version of the 27th Psalm, quickly, fervently:)

PHINEAS. "The Lord is my light and my salvation; whom shall I fear? When the wicked, mine enemies come upon me to eat my flesh, they stumble and fall...!" Etc.

(As JUNE overlaps with:)

JUNE. *(Overlapping, warning.)* Don't look at him. Don't meet his eye.

PHINEAS. "Hide not thy face from me, put not thy servant in danger; thou has been the help of my fleeessshhh—!

(PHINEAS groans and sinks to his knees — his stones are plaguing him again. JUNE grabs the gun out of his hand.)

GRAY. *(Concerned)* Pastor Wingfield?

PHINEAS. *(Doubled over in pain.)* Keep away from me!!!

JUNE. Go, go, go, go!

PHINEAS. *(Trying to crawl away.)* Somebody help me!

GRAY. Just hold still and let's have a look at you, sir.

JUNE. Are you crazy? Get on a horse and get out of here!

GRAY. Juney, just hold on a second. *(Checking PHINEAS.)* You tender here, are you?

PHINEAS. Jesus Almighty!

HOMER. *(Calls out.)* He's right over here!!

GRAY. Pastor, that stone's gonna have to come out.

(HOMER and CRUTCH enter with a fifth of whiskey and a shotgun, which CRUTCH levels at GRAY. Somebody might also have a hanging rope. PHINEAS is in mortal pain...he moans.)

HOMER. Good lord, he's killed the damn preacher!

JUNE. He hasn't killed anyone, Homer!

GRAY. I'm trying to help him!

CRUTCH. *(Levels his shotgun.)* Just get away from him.

PHINEAS. Oh, God — I'm dyin!

CRUTCH. Doc, I'd like nothin more than to shoot you right now.

(JUNE aims the small pistol at CRUTCH.)

JUNE. If you shoot him, I'll shoot you.

CRUTCH. Juney, what's gotten into you?

GRAY. Let's all of us just put the firearms down. If you kill me, he's gonna die, Mr. Collins.

JUNE. And so are you. So make your choice, and say your prayers.

PHINEAS. *(In excruciating pain.)* Oh, God, have mercy!!!

GRAY. I might be wrong, but I think his kidneys are backing up on him.

HOMER. You know how to save him?

GRAY. I do.

(HOMER looks at CRUTCH.)

CRUTCH. Then save him. And get out of town.

GRAY. June, get me a saddle blanket.

(JUNE rushes off stage.)

HOMER. I hope you know what you're doin.

(GRAY opens his carpet bag to look for his scalpel, which he keeps in a small leather case.)

GRAY. I think I've got everything I need with me.

CRUTCH. What're you rootin around for?

GRAY. Mr. Collins, would you point that damn gun at the ground before somebody gets his gonads blown off?!

(JUNE runs back on with a saddle blanket.)

    JUNE. Where you want it, Doc?
    GRAY. Just spread it out right here. *(To HOMER.)* Don't just stand there, son. Give me a hand with him, will you?
    PHINEAS. Don't move me!

(HOMER gets in position to help.)

    GRAY. Ready?
    PHINEAS. Oh, God...
    GRAY. One, two, three.

(PHINEA screams as they roll or lift him onto the blanket.)

    PHINEAS. Jeeeesus!!!!
    JUNE. Careful, now, careful.
    CRUTCH. Good lord, he's tender.
    HOMER. Are you gonna cut on him, Doc?
    GRAY. Crutch, give me that bottle.

(JUNE takes it from CRUTCH and gives it to GRAY.)

    JUNE. Here you go, Doc.
    GRAY. Pastor — now I'm gonna give you some whiskey. It'll help the pain, sir.
    CRUTCH. He ain't took a drink in his life.

(GRAY takes a drink himself.)

    GRAY. There's a first time for everything.

(He offers the whiskey to PHINEAS, who grabs the bottle and guzzles it.)

HOMER. *(After a moment.)* Just think of it as medicine, Preacher.

(Pause as they watch him drink.)

GRAY. That's it. *(PHINEAS keeps drinking. Finally stops.)* Now get his shirt open.
CRUTCH. He's got the damn bottle half emptied already.

(PHINEAS nearly passes out. GRAY takes the bottle from him.)

GRAY. Hold that lantern up, would you?

(CRUTCH still has the shotgun leveled at GRAY. HOMER holds the lantern up, too. GRAY pours some whiskey on his scalpel.)

JUNE. I hope to God this plague ain't in the bloodstream or you're gonna catch it for sure.
HOMER. How can you catch it? You're the one givin it, ain'tcha?
GRAY. Homer, I'm so damn stupid I thought you were smarter than that.

(He hands the bottle back to JUNE.)

GRAY. Here. Funnel another dose down him.
HOMER. It's gonna hurt like hell, Pastor.

(JUNE funnels another good, long drink of whiskey down PHINEAS.)

JUNE. Doc, have you ever done this procedure before?
GRAY. Only to dead people, Juney.
HOMER. *(Whispers to his Pastor.)* Keep drinkin.

(It's important that PHINEAS pass out. His body is turned slightly upstage, so the audience can't see his belly. GRAY takes a deep breath.)

GRAY. Alright. Whatever you do, don't let him start flailing around on me.
JUNE. You got a grasp on him?
HOMER. I hope to God so.
CRUTCH. Boy, that's quite a knife.
HOMER. Ain't it?
GRAY. *(Having trouble.)* Get a grip on yourself...*(GRAY says a quick prayer in Yiddish, then:)* Here we go, Pastor.

(The Pastor's undershirt, of course, is RED, pre-soaked with the color to signify BLOOD. GRAY makes his "incision" and turns away.)

GRAY. Oh, God...I'm gonna pass out...
HOMER. You can't quit on him now, Doc — you got him wide open!
JUNE. Here — take a drink, take drink!

(GRAY drinks.)

HOMER. Lord, would you look at that blood gushin?!

GRAY. Homer, go fetch us a pail of water.

HOMER. Right now?

GRAY. Don't make me beg you, son — do what I say!

CRUTCH. *(As HOMER takes off.)* Go to the well at the church.

(HOMER exits.)

GRAY. June, do you think you can follow instructions?

JUNE. I usually make em up as I go along, Doc.

GRAY. I'll make em up as you go along.

(GRAY hands the scalpel to JUNE.)

CRUTCH. Good lord, he's comin to!!!

PHINEAS. *(Screams)* Ahhhhhhhhh!!!

JUNE. Ahhhhhhhhh!!!

GRAY. Whiskey!

CRUTCH. Whiskey!

JUNE. Whiskey!

GRAY. Drink, drink, drink!

(GRAY holds the bottle to the preacher's lips. PHINEAS drinks again. Passes out again. GRAY pours a little more whiskey on the scalpel.)

GRAY. *(To JUNE.)* Are you alright?

JUNE. Uh huh. What do you want me to do?

GRAY. Do you see that darkish thing there?

JUNE. This'n?

GRAY. Don't cut that! You'll kill him!

JUNE. Calm down!

GRAY. Darkish-blue — right by the gall bladder. See it?

JUNE. Which one's the gall bladder?

(CRUTCH moves the lantern closer. He's set his shotgun down by now and is getting involved in the surgery.)

GRAY. *(Quietly, concentrating.)* There, June. Don't touch the mesenteric artery. You see that darkish mass?

JUNE. This thing right here?

GRAY. No, right beside it. Mr. Collins, there's a needle and thread in my coat pocket.

CRUTCH. Got it.

GRAY. Thread it.

JUNE. You want me to cut it?

GRAY. Wait a second...give me that whiskey...

(He dumps a little more whiskey in the incision.)

GRAY. There now — you see it?

JUNE. Yeah.

CRUTCH. Lord God, it's ugly...

GRAY. That's it...you're doing just fine...don't press the knife on it. Love with it...That's it...let the blade do your work.

JUNE. You got any tweezers?

GRAY. *(He has them ready.)* Here.

JUNE. Look at that thing — it's the size of a walnut...!

CRUTCH. No wonder it pains him.

GRAY. There we go — that's it — I'll pinch the vein for you. Keep your hand steady.

JUNE. I got the little devil!

(HOMER enters with a bucket in hand.)

HOMER. I gotcha that water, Doc.

CRUTCH. Good for you, Juney!

GRAY. *(To HOMER.)* Bring it on over. Give me that needle and thread, Mr. Collins.

CRUTCH. I'd say this calls for a drink.

GRAY. *(Re: the whiskey.)* Don't you dare waste a drop of that. *(Re: the water bucket.)* Dip a little water in there to rinse out the incision — then I'll close him up. *(JUNE does so.)* That's it. And now a little whiskey to kill off the germs. *(GRAY pours some "whiskey" on the surgical wound.)* Whiskey and water, June...whiskey and water's the key.

HOMER. I hate the taste of water.

GRAY. Water's the best thing to purify the system. You can't live on nothing but soda pop, Homer.

HOMER. I do.

JUNE. You're not half bad with that needle, Doc.

HOMER. I always thought sewin was kind of a female art.

JUNE. Just like repairin a ripped up old sofa...

(Pause. GRAY sews.)

GRAY. June, can you cut that thread for me? *(She does so.)* Thank you.

JUNE. You're welcome.

CRUTCH. You finished?

GRAY. *(Finishing)* Thank God...

HOMER. You did a fine job, Doctor Gray.

GRAY. No, she did a fine job. *(Then)* Let's just hope he lives through it.

(Everybody shakes everybody else's hand or pats them on the back.)

JUNE. I didn't think you had it in you, Doc.

HOMER. What do you know about that?

GRAY. Mr. Collins, I beg of you: Let me do an autopsy on Belva. Let me learn what I can from her, please.

CRUTCH. It ain't right to cut a dead person, Doc. I can't letcha do it. She's suffered enough as it is.

(There's no changing his mind.)

GRAY. Alright, let's get this man home to his bed. Mr. Collins, if you'll get his feet for me, please. And Homer, you prop up the middle.

JUNE. Careful now.

GRAY. Ready. Set...

(The three MEN lift PHINEAS and carry him off.)

CRUTCH. I'm too damned old for this.

GRAY. Try not to jostle him. Easy, boys.

JUNE. Good lord, this blanket's a mess.

CRUTCH. Hey, June bug, will you get my gun for me?

JUNE. Surely.

GRAY. Watch it now, watch your step...

(And they're gone. JUNE is alone on stage. She picks up the shotgun, and the water bucket or lantern. Then turns to face the theater:)

JUNE. After my father died, I felt so angry, and sad, and confused that I sat down and wrote a long letter to the Powers that Be. I wished for a doctor. I prayed for a healer. But I had no idea that the doctor I'd wished for was me.

(TINY and MAGGIE enter. They speak to the theater as JUNE exits.)

MAGGIE. The weather report is as follows:
TINY. First it got colder and then it got warm.
MAGGIE. The first sign of illness was fever.
TINY. I felt like my very soul was on a scavenger hunt to find God.
MAGGIE. You're gettin warmer and warmer and warmer and warmer.

(GRAY enters.)

GRAY. Let's have a look at your eyes, Tiny.
TINY. Why?
GRAY. Just look at me, please. Hold still.
TINY. You are the nicest individual...
GRAY. Pupils are dilated.
TINY. Dilated. What does that mean? Is that bad or good?
GRAY. I think you better lie down for a spell.
TINY. I don't have time to lie down — I need to look after my brother.
GRAY. Your brother's just fine. June's watching after him.
TINY. June's just a child! She can't barely look after herself.
GRAY. Let's just worry about you for right now.
MAGGIE. You're gettin warmer and warmer.

(LIGHTS change. TINY'S attitude changes. She is in pain.)

TINY. I don't know what's wrong with me./

MAGGIE. After the fever set in, the markings would blister. /

TINY. I feel like I could crawl out of my skin. /

GRAY. Let's check your vitals. /

TINY. No. Thank you. /

GRAY. I need to examine you, Tiny. I've got other people to see today.

TINY. I just want to get better. Don't you understand that?/

GRAY. We've got to get that damn fever down.

TINY. I'll change. I can change. I can be a new person —

GRAY. Tiny. /

TINY. —Whatever I'm doin, I'll change it, I swear— /

GRAY. I made a salve for you.

TINY. I'll change everything! /

GRAY. *(To the point.)* Tiny./

TINY. What?

GRAY. Hush up and sit down, right now.

TINY. I'm doin it — right now. I'm sittin, I'm hushin, I'm healin, I'm changin, I'm gonna be fine, ain't I? What in God's name are you doin to me?

GRAY. It's only a salve, Ma'am. /

TINY. It's burnin.

GRAY. Everything good for you has a price. Now hold still and just let me work on you. /

(She relaxes a tiny bit.)

TINY. You missed a spot. /

GRAY. Thank you. /

(JUNE brings on a basin and a wash cloth for GRAY.)

    MAGGIE. First Belva, then Tiny—
    JUNE. Then all across the countryside people began to take ill.

(Night. TINY is lying down now; fevered, trembling. GRAY tends to her; washing her forehead and arms with a cool, damp cloth. More TOWNSPEOPLE enter, becoming like a chorus of witnesses behind them, alternately commenting on TINY'S story, and caught up in their own.)

    TINY. What is happening to me?
    MAGGIE. You're gettin warmer—
    CRUTCH. *(Entering)* And warmer.
    TINY. I've got to get myself straight with the Lord.
    MAGGIE. And warmer—
    HOMER. *(Entering)* And warmer—
    TINY. I ain't ready to go yet.

(TINY sinks to her knees to make her final bargains with God during the scene below. Although GRAY is focused on TINY throughout this dying chapter, he is now part way across the stage, as the situation in intensity:)

    JUNE. Doctor Gray?
    HOMER. Doctor, I know it's late.
    TINY. I've got to take care of my brother. he don't even know how to cook.
    HOMER. Doctor, I'm worried.
    CRUTCH. I'm sorry to wake you.
    JUNE. Doc, Mr. Collins ain't well at all.

TINY. Oh, God...I have sinful thoughts in me.

JUNE. Just tell me how to take care of him, please.

TINY. Shameful things runnin through me like a river.

CRUTCH. I thought I told you to go fetch the doctor.

HOMER. Have you seen the doctor?

TINY. I mean to be better.

JUNE. Doc, she's been coughin up blood all night long.

MAGGIE. I can't get any nourishment down him.

TINY. I want to be healed.

JUNE. She just can't stop coughin.

TINY. Forgive me!

MAGGIE. Doctor, please.

TINY. Oh, God, forgive me!

JUNE. I don't know what to do for it!

HOMER. Doctor Gray?

CRUTCH. Doctor?

JUNE. There's so many people.

MAGGIE. I just hate to see him in pain.

HOMER. Doc, they need you to come by the house right away.

JUNE. My God, can't you do somethin for her?!

(We begin to slow down now, the tone changes...TINY has died.)

MAGGIE. You're gettin warmer:

CRUTCH. And warmer—

JUNE. And warmer—

HOMER. And warmer.

GRAY. I'm sorry...

(BELVA enters, extends a hand. TINY simply sits up, takes her hand and exits. If GRAY remains on stage, he is lost in his own dark thoughts throughout the following:)

MAGGIE. It was like as if the fevers turned into a fire that consumed every soul in its sight.

HOMER. Doctor Gray told us to burn everything that the sickness had ever had part in.

CRUTCH. As the weather grew colder and the darkness grew longer, fires were burnin all over the county.

HOMER. Fires and fever is all I recall.

MAGGIE. But into the midst of this illness —

CRUTCH. This terrible markin upon us, as if like a mark upon Cain —

MAGGIE. A life came upon us —

(REBEKAH enters with a swaddling blanket she holds close: this blanket is her newborn "baby". She sings a made-up lullaby to it, softly, sadly. There's a moment as the STORY-TELLERS hear a few lines of her song.)

REBEKAH. *(Sings)*
"Go to sleep, my baby; go to sleep, my love...
Go to sleep, my pretty little child, in the arms above..."

MAGGIE. *(Overlapping from "love")* A child is born.

HOMER. A beautiful—

CRUTCH. Beautiful—

MAGGIE. Perfect young baby.

JUNE. That's my little sister we're talkin about.

(REBEKAH continues to hum to her "baby" as the story continues. MAGGIE, HOMER, and JUNE exit.)

CRUTCH. The baby was born on a night when so many stars jeweled the sky, you just wanted to reach up with both hands and take a few home. *(Then:)* She was born on the same night I died.

(BELVA is waiting. They leave the stage together. GRAY crosses to REBEKAH.)

GRAY. Rebekah?...Rebekah, are you alright?
REBEKAH. I'm just fine.
GRAY. What about the baby?
REBEKAH. She's beautiful, Galen. She's just...perfect.
GRAY. Is she alright?
REBEKAH. She's not marked, if that's what you mean.

(This is huge news, just huge, but he reacts to it quietly.)

GRAY. Thank goodness. Thank goodness.
REBEKAH. She looks just like her pa.
GRAY. Every newborn looks like a constipated eskimo to me. *(Off REBEKAH'S smile.)* What're you naming her?
REBEKAH. You take her.
GRAY. Rebekah.
REBEKAH. Galen, I'm marked. I can't keep this child, even if I wanted to — which I think I do — I just can't. You know that as well as I do. Just take her, please.
GRAY. Becky.
REBEKAH. I can't bear to fall in love with her anymore than I already have.

(REBEKAH gives GRAY the "baby".)

REBEKAH. I want you to take her and take Juney, and leave.

GRAY. You want me to take both your children?

REBEKAH. Cross the river and never look back.

GRAY. No, Ma'am, I'm not gonna do that.

REBEKAH. *(Verging on tears.)* I don't want my children to die!

GRAY. Well, I'm not gonna leave you here to die alone.

REBEKAH. What good can you stayin here possibly do? — except to sacrifice that little baby and June! You don't know the cause, you don't know the cure — you don't know anything!

GRAY. For the first time in my life I know I'm a doctor. And I reckon a blind man could see my feelings for you.

REBEKAH. You think I don't want you to stay? You think I'm not terrified? If you stay here on my account, and if my children catch this and die, I swear to God I will never forgive you.

(The "baby" starts FUSSING. GRAY looks at REBEKAH, makes his decision.)

GRAY. I'm gonna give her to June and stay here and take care of you.

REBEKAH. You will do no such thing.

GRAY. Juney?? Hey June?

(The "baby" starts CRYING.)

JUNE. *(Enters with a bottle.)* Oh, for Pete's sake, she's just squallerin cause she's hungry, Doc. Just give her a bottle, that's all she wants.

GRAY. Here. Why don't you give her the bottle?

(JUNE takes the "baby", gives her the bottle.)

JUNE. Oh, stop your fussin. *(The "baby" does. There's a "moment" as REBEKAH watches her daughters together.)* There you go, that's a girl, that's a good baby...

GRAY. You know what I think?

JUNE. No, but I bet you're gonna tell me.

GRAY. I think she's taken a shine to you.

JUNE. I think she's got our Pa's eyes. Don't get me wrong — she's prettier than him —

REBEKAH. Thank the Lord.

JUNE. — but it's just like he's starin right back at me, Mama.

(MAGGIE and PHINEAS once again talk to the theater. Note: PHINEAS is still recovering from his surgery; he's weakened.)

MAGGIE. And so, in the fullness of time, June and her family walked down to the water's edge.

PHINEAS. As those of us left on the good ground of Shariton County gathered together that evenin to bury our dead —

MAGGIE. Those who were marked and those who were unmarked did part from each other.

(JUNE, the baby, REBEKAH and GRAY are downstage near the "boat". MAGGIE and PHINEAS remain upstage in tableau in the "graveyard". HOMER enters with a carpet bag that's filled with bottles of soda — although the audience must not hear them clinking yet or realize that's what he has in the bag.)

REBEKAH. Hello, Homer.

HOMER. Evenin, Miss Becky. Doc.

GRAY. Homer.

HOMER. Good golly, is that the new baby?

JUNE. Ain't she the prettiest thing you ever laid eyes on?

HOMER. *(Looking at JUNE.)* No.

JUNE. Hush up.

HOMER. What's her name anyway?

JUNE. I reckon I'll just call her Sister.

HOMER. Hey, little Sister.

REBEKAH. You three take care now.

JUNE. *(Fighting back tears.)* I'll write to you, Mama. I miss you already.

REBEKAH. I miss you, too, baby. Now go on. Get out of here, before I start cryin.

(REBEKAH and JUNE can't and don't touch because of the "mark", although they long to.)

HOMER. *(To GRAY.)* I ain't never been nowhere else. What is it like out there?

GRAY. You'll navigate.

HOMER. You're not comin with us, I take it?

GRAY. No, son, I mean to stay here.

JUNE. I'm not sayin goodbye to you.

GRAY. Good. I'm not saying goodbye to you either.

JUNE. *(Holds her hand out.)* Doctor Gray.

GRAY. *(Takes her hand.)* Doctor Muldoon. I trust that we'll meet again soon.

(GRAY kisses JUNE'S hand; then she kisses his hand.)

HOMER. I ain't never been in a boat before neither.

REBEKAH. Just mind your balance. You're gonna do fine.

(HOMER sets his carpet bag down before getting in the "boat" — we hear bottles CLINKING together.)

JUNE. What in the world do you have in there, Homer?
HOMER. Soda pop.
JUNE. Soda?
HOMER. You want one?
GRAY. *(Hands HOMER the bag.)* Homer.
HOMER. I figure I'm best off to be prepared, Doc.
JUNE. Here. You mind the baby. I'll do the honors.
HOMER. You want me to hold her?
JUNE. Get used to it, Homer.
HOMER. *(To the baby.)* Hello there.
REBEKAH. Goodbye now.
HOMER. Bye.
JUNE. *(Suddenly tearful.)* Mama? Oh, God, Mama??
REBEKAH. When she's old enough to understand, you tell little Sister I love you both. Now go on, June. You have to be strong now. Don't you ever look back.

(JUNE paddles them onto the RIVER as the LIGHTS isolate their "boat" in a gentle blue wash. GRAY and REBEKAH slowly back away from the "boat" and cross into the funeral. A very soft river sound might sneak in.)

PHINEAS. The river shone bright as a promise that night.
MAGGIE. And so, with the bright stars of evenin to serve as a guide, they cast themselves onto the water, and travelled off into the world.

PHINEAS. "Ashes to ashes."
REBEKAH/MAGGIE/GRAY. "Ashes to ashes."
PHINEAS. "And dust unto dust."
REBEKAH/MAGGIE/GRAY. "Dust unto dust."

(GRAY and REBEKAH look back toward the RIVER. JUNE continues to paddle with strength, slowly, elegantly...)

GRAY. *(Quietly)* Water...
PHINEAS. Sir?
GRAY. Maybe it's water.
MAGGIE. Well, Doc, it's a river.
GRAY. He doesn't drink water. I boil my water. June does what I do.
REBEKAH. She has since you got here.
GRAY. It's the simplest thing in the world.
PHINEAS. Water.

(They look toward the RIVER again...and JUNE glances back at them, too.)

HOMER. Juney?
JUNE. What, Homer?
HOMER. You heard what your mother said: Don't look back.
JUNE. But I want to remember.
HOMER. I know. But it'll just make you miss it all the more.
JUNE. Don't tell me you're already homesick.

(The LIGHT IS SLOWLY GROWING FAINTER on her mother and GRAY and the TOWNSPEOPLE, as if they're more and more distant. JUNE continues to paddle at the same steady rhythm.)

HOMER. I never knew a man could miss dirt so much. But I'll tell you somethin: I miss my farm, Juney, I really do. I miss my dirt.

JUNE. I have a baby and I'm a virgin. So don't complain, Homer.

HOMER. Didn't that happen to somebody else one time? *(After a beat.)* Juney?

JUNE. What, Homer?

HOMER. What do you think we might find out here?

JUNE. The rest of the world, I imagine.

(MUSIC, of course, has snuck in by now. The LIGHT on the grave-yard is fading to darkness as JUNE continues to paddle.)

HOMER. Well. It can't be as pretty as Gray, Indiana.

(LIGHTS FOCUS TIGHTER AND TIGHTER ON JUNE, until she is the only thing we see...)

JUNE. *(To the theater.)* June could not bear to look back on the pain or the beauty of her childhood again, but she never want-ed to forget — so at that very moment, under these very stars, and on this very river, she began to compose a story in her mind to tell her little Sister someday. So she'd understand that we all come from loss, and from love. And her story ended and began like this: Once upon a time there was a girl who looked remarkably like me.

(LIGHTS TO BLACK.)

THE END